U0022394

Tashi and the Demons
© Text, Anna Fienberg and Barbara Fienberg 1999
© Illustrations, Kim Gamble 1999
First published in 2000 by Allen & Unwin Pty Ltd., Australia
Chinese translation copyright © 2002 by San Min Book Co., Ltd.

•大喜說故事系列•

Tashi
and the
MAGIC BELL
大喜與奇妙鐘

Anna Fienberg
Barbara Fienberg 著

Kim Gamble 繪

柯美玲 譯

三民書局

'Look out, Tashi! Hide behind this tree,
quick!' Jack pulled Tashi down beside him.

「小心，大喜！躲在這棵樹後面，趕快！」傑克把
大喜拉到自己身邊。

'What is it?'

'Look, *there*.' Jack pointed to the **veranda** of number 42. An old man **leant** over the **balcony**. He had wild curly hair and a **cockatoo** on his shoulder. He didn't look very dangerous to Tashi. But then Tashi had seen a lot of evil and **calamitous** things in his time, it was true.

'That's Mr B. J. Curdle. He's always **pestering** me,' **hissed** Jack. 'I'm just walking home from school, right—like now, **minding** my own business—and out **dashes** old Curdle, stopping me and asking *how I am*.'

Tashi **frowned**. 'What's so terrible about that?'

「怎麼啦？」

「你看那邊，」傑克指著四十二號人家的長廊。有個老人正把身子探出陽臺。他的頭髮又亂又捲，肩膀上還站著一隻鳳頭鸚鵡。大喜覺得他沒什麼可怕的。不過大喜從小就見過許多邪惡、會引起災難的事物，所以在他眼中那個老人的確不算什麼。

veranda [və`rændə] 名 長廊

lean [lin] 動 身體前傾《over》

balcony [`bælkənɪ] 名 陽臺

cockatoo [`kɑkətu] 名 鳳頭鸚鵡

calamitous [kə`læmətəs] 形 引起災難的

「那是夏仁先生。他老是煩我，」傑克小聲地罵。「每次我從學校走回家，沒錯——就像現在一樣，邊走邊想事情——那老頭就突然衝出來攔住我，問我好不好。」

大喜皺起眉頭。「那有什麼好怕的？」

pester [`pɛstɚ] 勔 困擾
hiss [hɪs] 勔 小聲斥責
mind [maɪnd] 勔 想
dash [dæʃ] 勔 衝
frown [fraʊn] 勔 皺眉頭

'Well, he makes these dreadful homemade medicines from plants in his garden, and he wants to try them out on *me*! Once, I felt sorry for him—his cockatoo had a **limp**—so I went in. Instead of lemonade he gave me this thick yellow stuff to drink. He said it was **strengthening** medicine. Yuk!'

'And did it make you strong?'

'You've got to be kidding! That **mixture** made me weak as a baby—it tasted like **mashed** cockroaches. I felt like throwing up all the way home. The man's a **menace**!'

「喔，他用他園子裡種的植物提煉出很可怕的藥，還想拿我當實驗品！有一次我替他感到難過──他那隻鳳頭鸚鵡的腳跛了──所以我才進去他家。沒想到他不是請我喝檸檬汁，而是拿出一種黃黃稠稠的東西要我喝下去。還說那是大力藥。嗯！」

「那種藥有讓你變得更強壯嗎？」

「別開玩笑了！那藥水害我虛弱得像個小嬰兒──它嚐起來就像是搗碎的蟑螂餅。回家的路上，我一直好想吐。那傢伙是個危險人物！」

limp [lɪmp] 图 跛
strengthening [ˋstrɛŋθənɪŋ] 形 增強的
mixture [ˋmɪkstʃɚ] 图 藥水
mash [mæʃ] 動 搗碎
menace [ˋmɛnɪs] 图 危險的人

When the old man had gone back inside, and the two boys were walking home, Tashi said, 'What you need is a Magic **Warning** Bell, like the one we had in my village. It rang whenever danger was near.'

'Ooh, that *would* be **handy**. What did it look like?'

當老人走回屋裡，兩個小男孩也起身準備回家時，大喜說，「你需要的是一口奇妙鐘，就像以前我們村了裡的那個一樣。只要一有危險，它就會響。」

　　「哦，那樣的確方便多了。那個鐘長什麼樣子啊？」

warning [`wɔrnɪŋ] 形 警告的
handy [`hændɪ] 形 方便的

'Well, it was very old and beautiful, the most **precious** thing we had in the village. When dragons came over the mountain it would ring out, and once, when a giant **wandered** near, its clanging was so **deafening** that even people working in the fields had time to escape. Lucky for me, it rang the day the River Pirate arrived.'

Jack stopped on the path. 'Oh, I remember *him*—he was that really **fierce** pirate you tricked with a bag of fake gold.'

Tashi nodded. 'I had to, or I'd have been **carved** up like a turkey. But I always knew when he discovered it he would come back to get me.'

「嗯，那是口非常古老又美麗的鐘，是我們村子的寶貝。當龍從山的那邊爬過來時，它就會響。還有一次，一個巨人走近村子，它就叮噹叮噹地響得震耳欲聾，大聲到甚至連在田裡工作的人也有時間逃跑。我很幸運，河盜來的那一天，它也響了。」

傑克在小徑上停了下來。「哦，我記得他——他是那個被你用一袋假金子騙了的壞強盜。」

大喜點點頭。「我必須這麼做，不然我可能早就像火雞一樣被切成一塊一塊的了。可是我知道一旦被他發現，他一定會回來找我算帳。」

precious [ˋprɛʃəs] 形 寶貴的
wander [ˋwɑndɚ] 動 漫步
deafening [ˋdɛfənɪŋ] 形 震耳欲聾的
fierce [fɪrs] 形 凶惡的
carve [kɑrv] 動 把肉切開

13

Jack **shivered**. 'So what did he do?'

'Well, it was like this,' said Tashi. 'I was in the village **square** getting some water from the well when the bell **tolled** softly. It seemed to be ringing just for me.

傑克嚇得渾身發抖。「他怎麼報復？」

　　「這個嘛，事情是這樣的，」大喜說。「有一次，當我正在村子廣場的井邊打水時，那口鐘輕輕地響了起來，彷彿只是為我而響的。

shiver [ˋʃɪvɚ] 動 發抖

square [skwɛr] 名 廣場

toll [tol] 動（鐘）緩慢有規律地鳴響

'I stood there, **frozen**, trying to think. But all I could see in my mind was that Pirate, **stroking** the end of his **sword**. I **sipped** some water. That helped. I decided that the first place he'd look for me would be my house, so I dropped my **bucket** and ran to my cousin Wu, who lived high up on a hill overlooking the village.

'From Wu's front window I could see the River Pirate **tying up** his boat. Just the sight of him gave me the shivers. He was *huge*—the muscles in his arms were like boulders. I watched him **stride** along the **jetty**, turning into the road...he was heading straight for my house! My mother told him she didn't know where I was, but he **banged about** inside anyway, frightening her and my grandparents. He knocked a pot of soup off the fire and **kicked** over a table, then went charging about the village asking for me.'

「我站在那裡嚇呆了，努力想著可能會有什麼危險。可是我左想右想只想得到那個撫弄著刀柄的河盜。我喝了幾口水，頭腦總算稍微冷靜下來。我心想他第一個找的地方一定是我家，於是我扔下水桶，跑去找吳表弟，他住在高高的山坡上，可以俯瞰整個村子。

frozen [ˋfrozn̩] 形 嚇呆的
stroke [strok] 動 撫摸
sword [sɔrd] 名 刀
sip [sɪp] 動 啜飲
bucket [ˋbʌkɪt] 名 水桶

「從吳表弟家前面的窗戶，我可以看到河盜把他的船綁在岸邊。光是看到他，我就嚇得渾身發抖。他的身材高大──手臂的肌肉就像大圓石一樣。我看著他大步走過堤防，然後轉進馬路……直接就衝到我家去！我媽媽說她不曉得我人在哪裡，但他還是在屋子裡亂打亂敲，把我媽媽和爺爺奶奶都嚇壞了。他打翻爐子上的一鍋湯，踢翻了桌子，然後衝到村子裡四處打聽我的下落。」

tie up 繫緊
stride [straɪd] 動 跨步走
jetty [`dʒɛtɪ] 名 堤岸
bang about 到處喧鬧
kick [kɪk] 動 踢

19

Jack kicked a stone **ferociously**. 'They'd better not tell him where you were!'

'Well, a few villagers had seen me running up to Wu's house, but they all said they had no idea where I'd gone. Still, there was one little boy who didn't understand the danger I was in. He **skipped** up to the River Pirate calling, "Do you want to know where Tashi is? Well—" but at that moment three large women sat on him.

傑克狠狠地把一塊小石頭踢得老遠。「他們可千萬別說出你在哪裡！」

　　「嗯，有幾個村民看見我跑去吳表弟家，可是他們都說不知道我去哪兒了。不過，還是有個小男孩不知死活。他跳到河盜面前叫著，『你想知道大喜在哪裡嗎？嗯——』就在這個時候，三個胖婦人一屁股坐在他身上。

ferociously [fəˋroʃəslı] 副 狠狠地
skip [skɪp] 動 跳

'"Well *what*?" **growled** the River Pirate.
'"Well so do we," the women replied, and the
Pirate **scowled** and hurried on. He **searched** all
day, growing more and more angry. People ran
into their houses and locked the doors, but he
threw rocks at their windows and **tore** up their
gardens. That night, on his way back to the
boat, the River Pirate stole the Magic Bell.'

「『嗯，什麼？』那河盜對著他大吼。

　　「『呃，我們也想知道，』那幾個婦人回答他，河盜一臉不悅，又到別的地方找我。他找了一整天，越找越生氣。村裡的人都跑回家並把門鎖上，但是他卻拿石頭打破他們的窗戶，還破壞他們的花園。那天晚上，河盜在返回小船的路上，偷走了奇妙鐘。」

growl [graʊl] 動 吼叫

scowl [skaʊl] 動 沈下臉

search [sɝtʃ] 動 尋找

tear [tɛr] 動 撕裂，扯破《up》

'Oh no!' cried Jack.

'Oh yes!' said Tashi. 'The next morning, when they **noticed** that the bell was gone, the people were very **upset**. The Baron told everyone that it was my fault because I had tricked the River Pirate in the first place. People began to give me hard looks. They said that the bell had hung over the well since Time began and now, because of me, the village had lost its special warning. Some little children threw stones at me and their parents looked the other way. I felt so **miserable** I could have just sat down in a field and never got up.

「哦，不！」傑克叫了出來。

「是啊，沒錯！」大喜說。「隔天早上，村裡的人發現鐘不見了，大家都很沮喪。大地主跟每個人說都是我害的，因為是我先欺騙了那個河盜。於是村裡的人開始生氣地瞪我。他們說那口鐘從開天闢地以來就掛在那口井上面了，現在因為我，村子失去了最特別的警告聲。有些小孩子拿石頭丟我，他們的爸爸媽媽卻轉過頭去故意裝做沒看見。我好痛苦，很想乾脆就坐在地上，永遠不要起來。

notice [`notɪs] 勔 注意到
upset [ʌp`sɛt] 彤 沮喪的
miserable [`mɪzərəbl̩] 彤 悲慘的

'So I went to see Wise-as-an-Owl, to ask his **advice**. He was busy at his **workbench** when I walked in, filling jars with **herbs** and plants.

'"Ah, Tashi," he smiled as I came in. He looked at me for a moment. "You'd better help yourself to some **willowbark** juice over there."'

Jack **shuddered**. 'What's that? Does it taste like mashed cockroaches?'

「於是，我跑去請教聰明道人。我走進他家的時候，他正好在工作檯旁忙著把藥草和植物裝進瓶子裡。

　　「『哦，是大喜啊，』我走進去的時候，他對著我笑了一笑。他看了我一會兒。『你最好到那邊去倒些柳樹皮汁喝。』」

　　傑克一聽嚇壞了。「那是什麼東西？味道像不像被搗碎的蟑螂啊？」

advice [əd`vaɪs] 名 建議

workbench [`wɝk͵bɛntʃ] 名 工作檯

herb [hɝb] 名 藥草

willowbark [`wɪlo͵bɑrk] 名 柳樹皮

shudder [`ʃʌdɚ] 動 毛骨悚然

'No,' said Tashi. 'But it can **cure** headaches. I've learnt everything I know about plants and **potions** from Wise-as-an-Owl—he's an expert on the medicine plants of the mountain and forest. So I told him yes, I would have a **dose**, because I *did* have a pounding headache and a terrible problem.

'Of course Wise-as-an-Owl knew all about the River Pirate. He'd watched him **stamping** all over his herb garden out the front. "Go and face the **villain**, Tashi," he told me. "It will go better if *you* find *him* first."

「才不像呢，」大喜說。「柳樹皮汁能治好頭痛。聰明道人教了我很多關於植物和藥水的事——他是專門研究山林裡的藥草的專家。所以啦，我就說好，我會喝個一劑，因為我的頭砰砰砰地痛得不得了，而且我遇上了一個棘手的問題。

　　「聰明道人當然知道河盜來過。他看到他把前面院子裡的藥草通通踩壞了。『去對付那個壞蛋吧，大喜，』他告訴我。『你最好在他找到你之前先找到他。』

cure [kjʊr] 動 醫治
potion [ˋpoʃən] 名 藥水
dose [dos] 名（藥物等的一次）劑量
stamp [stæmp] 動 用力踩
villain [ˋvɪlən] 名 壞蛋

'He gave me two packets of special herbs to keep in my pocket. "Wolf's breath and jindaberry," he said. "Remember what I've taught you and mind how you use them."

'I thanked him and looked around for the last time at the plants and jars and pots of **dandelion** and **juniper** boiling on the stove. Then I **set out** for the city at the mouth of the river. There I would find the River Pirate.

「他給了我兩包特別的藥草，讓我放在口袋裡。『這是狼息草和金達莓，』他說。『記住我是怎麼教你的，用的時候要小心。』

　　「我向他道謝，最後再看看那些藥草、瓶瓶罐罐、還有正在爐子上熬煮的蒲公英和刺柏。然後我就出發前往河口的城市了。在那裡我一定可以找到河盜。

dandelion [ˋdændɪˌlaɪən] 名 蒲公英

juniper [ˋdʒunəpɚ] 名 刺柏

set out 出發

'I walked for two days, and as I **trudged** through forests and **waded** through streams, I thought about what I should say to him. On the last night, lying under the stars, I decided that I'd try to make a **bargain** with him. What I'd offer him would be fair, and would mean a big **sacrifice** for me!

'I had no trouble finding the River Pirate down in the **harbor**. He was sitting at the end of the jetty with his black-hearted crew.

You could hear them from **miles** away. They were **dangling** their legs over the side, passing a bucket of beer to each other and shouting and singing rude pirate songs at the tops of their voices. Every now and then they would tear great **hunks** of meat from a **freshly** roasted pig—stolen, you could be sure.'

「我走了兩天，一邊跋山涉水，一邊想著該怎麼跟他說。在抵達的前一個晚上，我躺在星空下，決定要跟他做個交易。我會給他相當優渥的條件，也就是說我必須做很大的犧牲！

「到了港口，沒兩下工夫我就找到了河盜。他和他那群黑心的同伴們正坐在碼頭的尾端。

trudge [trʌdʒ] 動 步履艱難地走
wade [wed] 動 徒步涉水
bargain [`bɑrgən] 名 交易
sacrifice [`sækrə,faɪs] 名 犧牲
harbor [`hɑrbɚ] 名 港口

幾哩外就聽得到他們的聲音。他們的腳在堤岸邊晃啊晃的，一桶啤酒傳過來、傳過去，一伙人一邊大聲唱著粗魯的海盜歌，還不時從一隻剛烤好的豬身上撕下大塊大塊的肉——那隻豬想也知道是偷來的。」

mile [maɪl] 名 哩
dangle [ˋdæŋgl̩] 動 搖晃
hunk [hʌŋk] 名（肉等的）厚切片
freshly [ˋfrɛʃlɪ] 副 剛剛才

'"There you are, you **treacherous** young devil!" the River Pirate **spluttered** when he saw me, **leaping** up and showering my face with greasy **gobbets** of pig. He grabbed my arm and **yanked** me toward him. His hand flew to his sword.

'"Wait!" I cried. "Listen!" I took a deep breath to stop my voice from trembling. Suddenly I had terrible doubts that a River Pirate could care about people being fair or making sacrifices, but it was the only idea I'd had. "If I work for you for a year and a day," I said boldly, "will you give back the bell?"

「『原來你在這兒啊，你這個奸詐的小鬼！』河盜看到我時跳了起來，很快地說出這句話，還把油膩膩的豬肉噴在我臉上。他一把抓住我的手臂，用力把我拉到他面前，另一隻手則飛快地伸過去拿刀。

　　「『等一下！』我大叫一聲。『聽我說！』我深深吸了一口氣，好讓說話時聲音不要發抖。突然間，我開始懷疑起河盜會不會在乎公不公平或犧不犧牲，但當時我也沒其他法子可想了。『如果我為你工作一年又一天，』我大膽地說，『你會把鐘還給我嗎？』

treacherous [`trɛtʃərəs] 形 奸詐的
splutter [`splʌtɚ] 動 急促地說
leap [lip] 動 跳《up》
gobbet [`gɑbɪt] 名（肉的）一塊
yank [jæŋk] 動 用力拉

'The River Pirate just laughed. He threw back his great bony head and roared, "I will keep you for *ten* years and a day—and the bell as well!" Then the crew grabbed me and **tossed** me into the boat.

'By sunset we'd set sail. When the first star **glittered** in the sky, the cook told me to go down into the **galley** and start chopping mountains of fish and vegetables. And every day after that I had to do the same arm-aching jobs. The cook was **spiteful** and the work was hard and boring—except when it was frightening. Like the time another pirate ship **attacked** us.'

「河盜聽了哈哈大笑。他把他那尖尖的火頭往後一甩，大吼著說，『我要把你留個十年又一天——那口鐘也一樣！』然後，那群河盜就抓住我，並把我丟進船裡。

　　「我們在太陽下山的時候出海。當天上出現第一顆星星的時候，廚子叫我到下面的廚房去切成堆的魚和菜。從那天以後，我每天都得做同樣的工作，做得我手臂痠死了。那個廚子的心眼很壞，而我的工作是既辛苦又無聊——有時還會讓我提心吊膽。就像那次別艘海盜船來攻擊我們的時候一樣。」

toss [tɔs] 動 丟
glitter [`glɪtɚ] 動 閃閃發亮
galley [`gælɪ] 名 （船的）廚房
spiteful [`spaɪtfəl] 形 惡毒的
attack [ə`tæk] 動 攻擊

'*Enemy* pirates?' cried Jack. 'What did you use as a weapon—your kitchen knife?'

'Well,' said Tashi, 'it was like this. One moonless night, a swarm of **bawling**, yelling-for-blood pirates **sprang** onto our boat. They took us completely by surprise. Where could I hide? I glanced frantically around the boat and spied a big coil of rope. I **scuttled** over and buried myself in the rope just as the enemy Captain bounded up. He was barking orders and threats like a mad dog when he suddenly caught sight of the River Pirate. Swiping at the air with his sword, he gave a vicious battle cry—and tripped over me! *Wah*! I shivered when I looked up into his face, but he didn't hesitate for a moment. He picked me up as if I were just a weevilly old **crust** and **flicked** me overboard.

「別的海盜來攻擊？」傑克大叫。「你拿什麼來當武器——菜刀嗎？」

「這個嘛，」大喜說，「事情是這樣的。在一個沒有月亮的晚上，一大群海盜又吼又叫、殺氣騰騰地跳上我們的船，把我們全都嚇了一大跳。我能躲在哪兒呢？我發了瘋似地看看船上有沒有可以躲藏的地方，最後看到一大綑繩子。我急急忙忙地跑過去，就在敵方的頭頭跳上船的那一刻，趕緊把自己藏在繩子堆裡。那傢伙像隻瘋狗似地發號施令、恐嚇威脅。突然間，他看到了那個河盜。他開始拿著劍在空中揮舞，口裡還發出喊殺聲——然後整個人跌在我身上！哇！我看到他的臉時嚇得渾身發抖。他想也不想就把我拎了起來，好像在拎一塊長滿象鼻蟲、又臭又硬的麵包皮一樣，然後把我丟進海裡。

bawl [bɔl] 動 大叫

spring [sprɪŋ] 動 跳（過去式 sprang [spræŋ]）

scuttle [`skʌtl̩] 動 倉皇跑走

crust [krʌst] 名 麵包皮

flick [flɪk] 動 輕彈

'Lucky for me there was a rope **ladder** hanging from the side of the boat. I grabbed it and **swung** down, **clinging** onto the last **rung** as I dangled in the black and icy water.

「還好船的旁邊掛著一個繩梯。我抓住繩梯，搖搖晃晃地往下爬，緊抓住最後一級繩梯，半掛著泡在又黑又冰的海水裡。

ladder [ˋlædɚ] 名 梯子

swing [swɪŋ] 動 搖擺（過去式 swung [swʌŋ]）

cling [klɪŋ] 動 緊緊抓住

rung [rʌŋ] 名（梯子的）階梯，橫木

'My fingers were **stiffening** with cold and it was hard to hang onto the fraying strands of rope. Something **slithery** kept twining around my legs! I kicked hard and looked down into the dark waves. A giant **octopus** was staring up at me, its **tentacles groping** for my ankle. Then, to my horror, I felt my shoe being sucked from my foot!

'At that very moment, just when it seemed that my mother would never see her precious boy again, I heard the River Pirate and his men bellowing out their song of victory. I could hear the dreadful splash as enemy pirates were thrown over the side.

「我的手指都凍僵了，很難抓住那早已磨損的繩子。我感覺到有個滑溜溜的東西一直纏著我的腳！我用力一踢，然後低頭睜大眼睛看著黑黑的海浪。一隻大章魚正瞪著我看，它的觸手纏住了我的腳踝。緊接著，嚇死我了，我感覺到腳下的鞋被吸走了！

「就在那個時候，眼看我媽媽再也見不到她的寶貝兒子的時候，我聽到河盜一伙人高聲唱出勝利之歌。接著，我聽到嚇人的撲通、撲通、撲通聲，敵人一個個被丟進海裡了。

stiffen [`stɪfən] 動 僵直

slithery [`slɪðərɪ] 形 滑溜溜的

octopus [`ɑktəpəs] 名 章魚

tentacle [`tɛntəkl̩] 名 觸鬚

grope [grop] 動 摸索

45

'Oh, how wet and **wretched** I was when I climbed back into the boat. But all I got was the River Pirate's **ranting fury**. "Why didn't that **mangy** magic bell ring to warn us?" he shouted, as he wiped the blood of an enemy pirate from his eye. "'It only rings for the place where it belongs," I told him, and he scowled so deeply that his **eyebrows** met in the middle.

「哦，當我慘兮兮地爬上船的時候，我全身濕透。但是，迎接我的卻是河盜的怒吼。『那個髒兮兮的鐘為什麼沒有發出聲音來警告我們？』他一邊大吼大叫，一邊從眼睛上擦掉敵人的血。

「『它只會為它歸屬的地方而響，』我告訴他，而他聽了之後非常不高興，眉頭都皺在一塊兒了。

wretched [`rɛtʃɪd] 形 可憐的
rant [rænt] 動 咆哮
fury [`fjʊrɪ] 名 狂怒
mangy [`mendʒɪ] 形 髒的
eyebrow [`aɪ,braʊ] 名 眉毛

'The next morning, I saw three pirates **racing** up to the **deck** to be sick over the side. By afternoon two more men and the cook looked quite green. They **wobbled** around as if their legs were made of noodles. As our village came into sight, I said to the River Pirate, "If I can cure your men of their sickness, will you let me go?"

'"No!" **snarled** the Pirate, but just then he bent over and **clutched** his stomach.

「第二天早上，我看到三個河盜急忙跑到甲板上對著海水嘔吐。到了下午，另外兩個人和廚子的臉色也開始發青。那些河盜走起路來都搖搖晃晃的，兩條腿就像是麵條做的一樣。當船快開到我們村子的時候，我對河盜說，『如果我能治好你的手下，你會放我走嗎？』

「『想都別想！』河盜大吼大叫，但就在這個時候，他彎下腰，抱住了肚子。

race [res] 動 急忙跑到
deck [dɛk] 名 甲板
wobble [`wɑbl̩] 動 搖晃
snarl [snɑrl] 動 吼著說
clutch [klʌtʃ] 動 緊抱著

"Aaargh, I'm dying...Go on then, but be quick," he **gasped**.

'I slipped down to the galley where I had hidden my packets of medicine plants. Quickly I threw some into a pot and boiled them up.

'The men only needed a few mouthfuls each before they stopped rolling about on the deck and sat up. One even smiled. The River Pirate was hanging over the side of the boat like a piece of limp **seaweed**, but he turned his head and begged for me to hurry.

'"And will you give me back the bell as well?" I asked him. The River Pirate **ground** his teeth. I **tilted** the pot a little. "I hope I don't **spill** these last few spoonfuls," I worried.

『啊，我快死了……去把藥拿來吧，動作快點，』他痛得喘不過氣來。

　　「我溜到下面的廚房去，那裡藏著我的藥草包。我急忙把一些藥草丟進鍋子裡煮。

　　「那些人只喝了幾口藥，就不再在甲板上打滾，一個個坐了起來。有一個甚至還笑了起來呢。河盜則像根軟趴趴的海草掛在船邊，他勉強轉過頭來，拜託我趕快拿藥給他。

　　「『那你會把鐘還給我嗎？』我問他。河盜氣得咬牙切齒。我把鍋子稍微傾斜。『希望我不會把最後這幾湯匙的藥灑到地上，』我假裝擔心地說。

gasp [gæsp] 勔 氣喘吁吁
seaweed [ˋsiˌwid] 名 海草
grind [graɪnd] 勔 磨（過去式 ground [graʊnd]）
tilt [tɪlt] 勔 使…傾斜
spill [spɪl] 勔 灑

'"Ah, take the bell, take it. It doesn't work anyway," the River Pirate hissed.

'And so that's how I came back to the village with the magic bell.'

Tashi looked at Jack and laughed. 'Do you **realize** we've walked right past your house and mine?'

'Well,' said Jack, **grinning**, 'come back to my place and have a glass of lemonade. Or we could always **call in** on Mr Curdle if you'd prefer...But tell me, what happened when you got home?'

「『啊，把鐘拿去，拿去。反正留著也沒用，』河盜虛弱地說。

「於是我就帶著奇妙鐘回村子去了。」

大喜看著傑克，哈哈哈地笑了起來。「你有沒有發現你家和我家都已經過了？」

「哦，」傑克也笑了出來，「到我家來喝杯檸檬汁吧。或者，你願意的話，我們也可以去拜訪夏仁先生……可是你得告訴我，你回家後發生了什麼事？」

realize [`riə,laiz] 勔 認清，明白

grin [grɪn] 勔 露齒而笑

call in 順道拜訪

'The villagers all crowded around, welcoming me and saying they were sorry for their **harsh** words. But when I took the bell out of the **sack**, there was a great shout and people threw their hats in the air. We hung the bell back on its **hook** over the well. And then—something that had never happened before—it gave a **joyful peal**!'

「村民們全都圍過來迎接我，並為他們之前的重話向我道歉。當我從袋子裡把鐘拿出來的時候，現場響起一陣歡呼聲，大伙兒高興地把帽子丟向空中。我們把鐘掛回那口井上的鉤子，這時——發生了一件前所未見的事——那口鐘居然發出快樂的響聲！」

harsh [hɑrʃ] 形 嚴厲的

sack [sæk] 名 袋子

hook [hʊk] 名 鉤子

joyful [`dʒɔɪfəl] 形 快樂的

peal [pil] 名 （鐘的）響聲

'Gee,' said Jack, 'wasn't it lucky that the pirates
got sick so that they needed your medicine!'
Tashi smiled. 'I think Wise-as-an-Owl would
tell you that luck had nothing to do with it.
Sometimes medicines that make you sick are
almost as useful as those that make you well.'
'Aha!' said Jack, giving Tashi a knowing look,
and they leapt up the steps of Jack's house, two
at a time.

「哇，」傑克說，「真幸運，碰巧那些海盜病了，沒有你的藥不行！」

　　大喜笑了一笑。「我想聰明道人會告訴你這跟幸不幸運沒有關係。有時候藥能治病，但有時候藥也會害人生病。」

　　「啊哈！」傑克邊說邊給大喜一個「我明白」的表情，然後兩個人就跳上傑克家的階梯，一步跨兩階地跑了上去。

●中英對照●

探索英文叢書·中高級

嗨！我是大喜，
我常碰到許多有趣的事情唷！
想知道我的冒險故事嗎？

來自遠方的大喜／大喜愚弄噴火龍／大喜智取巨人／大喜與強盜
大喜妙計嚇鬼／前進白虎嶺／大喜與精靈／大喜與被擄走的小孩
大喜巧鬥巫婆／大喜妙懲壞地主／大喜勇退惡魔／大喜與奇妙鐘
大喜與大臭蟲／大喜與魔笛／大喜與寶鞋／大喜與算命仙

共 16 本，每本均附 CD

•中英對照•

探索英文叢書‧中高級

波波 唸翻天系列

你知道可愛的小兔子也會 "碎碎唸" 嗎？

波波就是這樣。

他將要告訴我們什麼有趣的故事呢？

波波的復活節／波波的西部冒險記／波波上課記
我愛你，波波／波波的下雪天／波波郊遊去
波波打球記／聖誕快樂，波波／波波的萬聖夜

共 9 本，每本均附 CD

探索英文叢書・中高級　　中英對照，每本均附 CD

全新的大喜故事來囉！
這回大喜又將碰上什麼樣的難題呢？
讓我們趕快來瞧瞧！

Anna Fienberg & Barbara Fienberg／著
Kim Gamble／繪　王盟雄／譯

最新
出版

大喜與寶鞋

大喜的表妹阿蓮失蹤了！
為了尋找阿蓮，
大喜穿上了飛天的寶鞋。
寶鞋究竟會帶他到哪裡去呢？

最新
出版

大喜與算命仙

大喜就要死翹翹了！？
這可不妙！
盧半仙提議的方法，
真的救得了大喜嗎？

國家圖書館出版品預行編目資料

大喜與奇妙鐘／Anna Fienberg,Barbara Fienberg著;
　Kim Gamble繪;柯美玲譯.－－初版一刷.－－臺北
市；三民，民91
　　面；公分－－(探索英文叢書.大喜說故事系列;12)
中英對照
ISBN 957-14-3621-6　(平裝)
　1.英國語言－讀本

805.18

ⓒ　大喜與奇妙鐘

著作人　Anna Fienberg　Barbara Fienberg
繪　圖　Kim Gamble
譯　者　柯美玲
發行人　劉振強
著作財
產權人　三民書局股份有限公司
　　　　臺北市復興北路三八六號
發行所　三民書局股份有限公司
　　　　地址／臺北市復興北路三八六號
　　　　電話／二五〇〇六六〇〇
　　　　郵撥／〇〇〇九九九八——五號
印刷所　三民書局股份有限公司
門市部　復北店／臺北市復興北路三八六號
　　　　重南店／臺北市重慶南路一段六十一號
初版一刷　中華民國九十一年四月
編　號　S 85606
定　價　新臺幣壹佰柒拾元整
行政院新聞局登記證局版臺業字第〇二〇〇號

有著作權·不准侵害

ISBN　957-14-3621-6　(平裝)

網路書店位址：http://www.sanmin.com.tw